Another Point of View

FRIENDS AT THE END

by Dr. Alvin Granowsky

illustrations by Normand Chartier

D1403856

STECK-VAUGHN
COMPANY
ELEMENTARY • SECONDARY • ADULT • LIBRARY

2

You wouldn't think that a slow poke tortoise could beat a speedy hare like me, would you? Well, we all know he did. You just might not know how. Losing to that tortoise was the best thing that ever happened to me. I lost the race, but I won something else. Let me tell you about it.

Since I was very young, I have been one
speedy little hare. My family found out early how
quick I was. One sunny day, we went on a picnic
at the park. Mama Hare set me down just for a
minute to unpack our lunch. Before she knew it,
I had *zipped* to the other end of the pond.

"Where is Little Hare?" Mama Hare asked when she didn't see me on the blanket.

Papa Hare looked around. "My goodness, is that Little Hare way down there? How did he get there so fast?" he asked.

Soon, the word about my speed spread
to the other animals. "Have you seen how
fast Little Hare hops along?" they would ask
one another. "He's quicker than lightning!"

All the speedy animals wanted to race me.
The fox, the deer, and the squirrel each took
a turn.

"The hare wins again!" the lion would roar.

It felt great to be the winner. I'm afraid I just didn't think about how the other animals felt about losing.

After a while, the other animals stopped playing with me. "What's wrong?" I wondered. "We always have so much fun racing, don't we? I'm really fast, aren't I?" Well, fast or not, I had no friends. So I was very sad and lonely during my little bunny years.

9

Then one day, I was hopping by myself across the grasslands when I came upon the tortoise. He was chatting and laughing with some other animals.

"That tortoise sure has a lot of friends," I thought. "He's such a slow poke. But everyone still seems to like him."

When I saw all those animals having fun together, I felt even more lonely. I wanted to play, too. So I challenged the tortoise to a race. "Tortoise," I said, "can you imagine how you would do in a race against me?"

That little tortoise had spunk. He held his
head up high in the air and said, "I'll race you
anytime and any place!"

13

I laughed at the tortoise. The other animals turned their backs to me. "Don't worry about that hare," the raccoon said to the tortoise. "All he cares about is winning. He only thinks of himself."

"Be here at sunrise tomorrow," said the lion.
"The tortoise will race you then."

I walked home alone while the tortoise and
his friends played. I stayed up the whole night
thinking about what the raccoon said about me.
Could it be true? Did I only care about winning?
Was that why I had no friends?

The next morning, I was still upset. But the race began as planned. I took off like a flash when the lion roared, "Get ready, get set, go!" I wanted to get the race behind me. Then, halfway down the field, I looked back and saw the tortoise not far from the starting line.

Instead of feeling happy about winning, I felt sorry for the tortoise. It really wasn't right for me to ask him to race. After all, I am the *fastest* animal around, and he is the slowest. I began to think about how someone else might feel.

19

I didn't know what to do. I couldn't just stop
in the middle of the race. I closed my eyes to
think. Because I had been awake all night
worrying, I fell fast asleep.

I guess I slept so long that the tortoise had
passed me by. As he was about to cross the
finish line, the cheers of his friends woke me
up. I raced as fast as I could to win, but I was
too late. For the first time ever, I knew how it
felt to lose.

"Well, I still won't have any friends," I thought. "Now everyone will think I'm a loser."

That's not what happened at all. The other animals were very happy for the tortoise. But they also cared about me.

Even the tortoise tried to make me feel better. He put his arm around me and said, "Maybe next time!"

Well, I learned a lesson that I'd like to pass on to you. I used to think that I had to win all the time to have friends. Now I know that I can lose and still have friends. To have friends, I have to care about others. But you already knew that, didn't you?

Another Point of View

The Tortoise and the Hare

retold by Dr. Alvin Granowsky
illustrations by Delana Bettoli

STECK-VAUGHN
COMPANY
ELEMENTARY • SECONDARY • ADULT • LIBRARY

nce upon a time, there was a hare who could run very fast. In fact, the hare ran so fast that he was just a blur as he dashed over the hills and through the trees.

The hare liked to boast about his speed.
"I am the fastest runner in all the land," he
would often say to the other animals.

"Look around as far as you can see. You
won't find any animal that can run as fast as
I can."

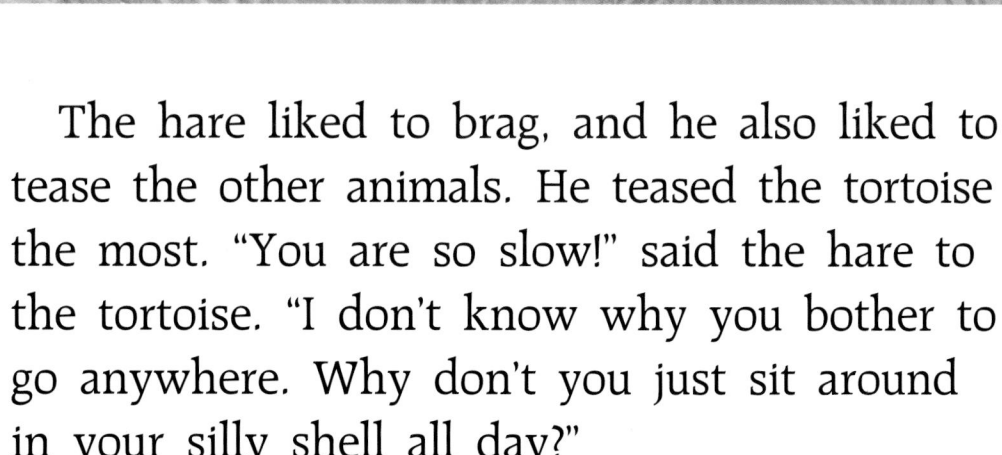

The hare liked to brag, and he also liked to tease the other animals. He teased the tortoise the most. "You are so slow!" said the hare to the tortoise. "I don't know why you bother to go anywhere. Why don't you just sit around in your silly shell all day?"

The tortoise grew tired of the hare's talk. "I may be slow, but I get where I want to go," said the tortoise.

The hare teased on. He said to the other animals, "Wouldn't it be funny to see the tortoise and me in a race?"

The tortoise spoke up. "Let's race to the end of the field," he said.

The hare laughed so hard that he cried.
"You want to race **me**?" he asked the tortoise.
He called to the other animals. "Tortoise
wants a race. Can you believe that? You can
all watch me win."

The other animals were tired of the hare's boasting, too. They knew that the tortoise was a fine animal who just happened to move slowly. There was no reason for the hare to be so unkind.

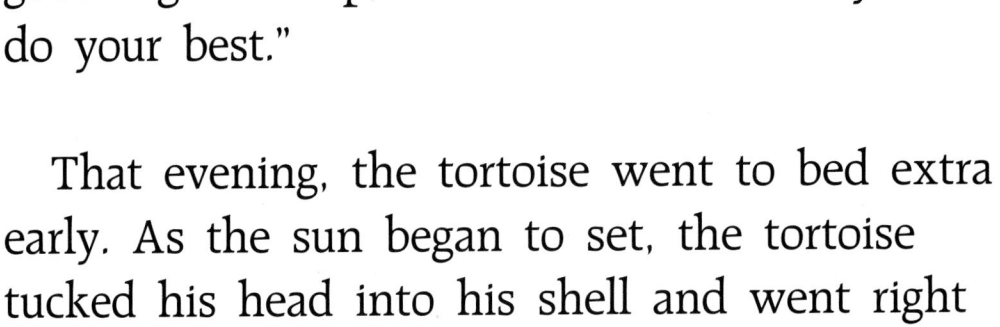

The race was set for early the next morning.
The lion would be the judge. "Be sure to get a
good night's sleep," said the lion. "Then you'll
do your best."

That evening, the tortoise went to bed extra
early. As the sun began to set, the tortoise
tucked his head into his shell and went right
to sleep.

It was almost time for the sun to rise, though, before the hare went to sleep. He stayed up and **played**. "I would much rather have fun than rest," he said. "Besides, I can beat the tortoise in a race without even trying."

The next morning, the tortoise was ready for the race. The hare was ready, too, but he was a bit sleepy. He could not stop yawning.

As the animals gathered around to watch the start of the race, they cheered for the tortoise.

The tortoise and the hare took their places on the starting line. The lion said, "Get ready, get set, go!" The race was on! The hare took off in a **flash**. He was far down the field before the tortoise had taken his first full step.

The race went on just as it had started.
The hare zoomed along, and the tortoise took
one steady step after another.

"I'm so far ahead," thought the hare. "I have
nothing to worry about. Winning will be easy."

"I'm doing my best," thought the tortoise.
"I can just keep taking one step at a time. I'll
get to the end of the field just as I wanted."

At the halfway mark, the hare felt tired. He turned around to see how far behind the tortoise was. The hare saw only a speck in the distance. The hare rubbed his sleepy eyes and yawned. "I think I'll take a little rest. I have plenty of time because that slow poke tortoise will take all day."

Soon the hare was fast asleep. But the tortoise was moving quietly toward the end of the field.

The hare snoozed for some time. When he woke up, he could see the tortoise about to cross the finish line!

As fast as his powerful legs could go, the hare raced to catch up. It was too late. The tortoise had crossed the finish line.

"The tortoise wins the race!" shouted the lion. The animals cheered as they danced around their friend. Then the lion said, "Here we have learned an important lesson."

All the animals gathered to listen as the lion said,
"Fast and speedy
May be great,
But slow and steady
Won **this** race."